THIS SWEET PICKLES® BOOK BELONGS TO

In the world of *Sweet Pickles,* each animal gets into a pickle because of an all too human personality trait.

This book is about Positive Pig who is absolutely sure that no matter what happens, it's all for the best.

Books in the Sweet Pickles Series:

Library of Congress Cataloging in Publication Data

Hefter, Richard.
    Pig thinks pink.

    (Sweet Pickles series)
    SUMMARY : Pig is positive everything will be all
right, even when everything is going all wrong.
    [1. Pigs—Fiction] I. Title. II. Series.
PZ7.H3587Pi   [E]   78-9581
ISBN 0-03-042051-2

Printed in the United States of America

Weekly Reader Books' Edition

Weekly Reader Books presents

PIG
THINKS PINK

Written and illustrated
by Richard Hefter
Edited by Ruth Lerner Perle

Holt, Rinehart and Winston · New York

Pig was climbing up a ladder in the middle of Main Street one morning. Her arms were full of brushes and tools and cans of paint.

Walrus came walking down the street. "Look out, Pig!" cried Walrus. "You'll fall and hurt yourself."

"No I won't," smiled Pig. "Ladders are very safe if you are careful. And I'm careful, and I'm busy too."

"What are you doing up there, anyway?" moaned Walrus. "Aren't you worried? Aren't you afraid of heights?"

"Oh Walrus," laughed Pig, "no, I'm not worried. No, I'm not afraid. Yes, I have lots to do. Yes, I'm very busy. Yes, I'm in charge of the big picnic and YES it's today."

"I didn't know the big picnic was today," sighed Walrus.

"Of course you didn't," giggled Pig. "I just invented it."

"But how can you invent a picnic," groaned Walrus, "and who put you in charge?"

"It's easy to invent a picnic," laughed Pig. "All you have to do is wake up one morning and look out the window and say to yourself, 'WOW! What a great morning for the big picnic!' Then you gather all the things you need for a terrific picnic and that puts you in charge."

"But Pig," wailed Walrus, "suppose nobody comes. And what if you forget the napkins? And where are the tables? And who is bringing the pickles? There are so many things to worry about when you are put in charge."

"Stuff and nonsense!" smiled Pig, as she started to paint red stripes on the side of the bank. "Who ever heard of anyone not coming to a big picnic? Everyone will come. And someone will bring the napkins and the tablecloths and the tables and someone will bring the food and someone else will bring the drinks and I will make the decorations. It will be the best big picnic that anyone in town has ever seen!"

"Oh dear, oh my," moaned Walrus softly. And he shuffled around and nodded his head.

"What's the matter now?" asked Pig. "You're always worried about something."

"Why aren't we in the park?"groaned Walrus. "Picnics are always in the park."

"Anyone can have a big picnic in the park," laughed Pig. "This picnic will be on Main Street. It's going to be the greatest picnic the town has ever seen. Folks will come from miles around. They'll be talking about it for months to come. Why, they might even call it the Great First Annual Pig Big Picnic. I'll be famous, and everyone will be so happy. We'll all have such wonderful fun!"

"But Pig," cried Walrus, "how can you call it a picnic if you didn't bring any food? And aren't you worried that someone will catch you painting stripes on the side of the bank?"

"Oh bother," smiled Pig. "Each person who comes to the picnic will bring a little food and the paint is only watercolor. We can wash it off after the picnic. Now stop worrying and come help me."

Pig and Walrus painted red stripes all over the side of the bank. Then they hung up red crepe paper streamers and set up a big sign that said:

WELCOME TO THE BIG PICNIC.

They waited. And waited. And waited. Nobody came by. Nobody brought food.

"I'm worried," moaned Walrus. "Nobody seems to be coming to our picnic."

"Don't worry, Walrus," said Pig. "It's a beautiful day and it's great fun just sitting here waiting for the picnic to begin and knowing that all our work is done and all we have to do is sit around and enjoy ourselves."

"It's a cloudy day," grumbled Walrus, "and I don't think anyone else will come to our picnic."

"You worry too much!" laughed Pig. "Look, here comes Goose."

"Hello, Pig and Walrus," mumbled Goose as she walked by, "what's going on?"

"Why, it's the Great First Annual Big Picnic!" shouted Pig. "And everyone's invited—come one, come all—we'll all have fun, HOORAY!"

"A picnic?" yawned Goose. "That sounds nice. Where is it going to be?"

"Why, right here!" laughed Pig. "You're right in the middle of it. WHOOPEE!"

"I don't see any food," sighed Goose, "and there aren't any tables either."

"It's all right," smiled Pig. "All that stuff will be coming later. It will be the best picnic the town has ever seen. Everyone will bring something and we'll all have a great time."

"Oh," said Goose, "a bring something picnic. Well, I'd love to come but I'm very tired now and I was just on my way home to rest. Maybe I'll come back later."

Goose shuffled off down the street.

"You see," groaned Walrus. "Nobody is going to come to this old picnic and we'll just sit here all alone and it will be so sad and lonely and..."

"Stop sniffling, Walrus," smiled Pig. "I tell you this will be a fantastic picnic and we will all have a great time! Just wait and see!"

They waited. And waited.

Yak drove by and said he would love to come to the picnic if only he didn't have to work today.

Rabbit walked over and said that he couldn't come to the picnic because he was too busy, and he told Pig and Walrus to make sure they removed the paint from the side of the bank before opening time on Monday.

Everybody was sorry they didn't know about the picnic before. Hippo was too busy jogging. Moose and Lion were on their way to the movies. Camel had to fix her truck. Quail was due at the library. Stork had mail to sort. Nightingale shrieked, "I won't come to your old picnic! Nyaaah!"

"Oh woe," groaned Walrus, "this is the worst thing that ever happened. Nobody will come to this picnic. We'll be all alone."

"Don't cry, Walrus," smiled Pig. "You worry too much. It doesn't matter if no one else comes to our picnic. I don't like big picnics, anyway. Too much mess and trouble with a big picnic."

"But Pig," sniffled Walrus.

"That's right," laughed Pig. "There's nothing nicer or sweeter than a lovely little picnic for us. Why, we'll eat a great picnic lunch. Then we can play ball or tag or just relax in the sun."

"But Pig," snuffled Walrus.

"I can see it now," giggled Pig. "Maybe we can fly kites or make necklaces out of flowers and leaves. We can watch grasshoppers and sunbathe. Small picnics are the best!"

"But Pig," moaned Walrus, "it just started to rain."

The rain poured down. The crepe paper got soggy and started to run. The red stripes on the side of the bank started to melt off. Watery pink goo was everywhere.

"Oh, oh, snuffle, moan," cried Walrus. "Just look at this mess. Now our lovely little picnic for just the two of us is ruined. What a mess, how awful! Why do these things always happen to me? Oh, sniffle, groan."

"Isn't this wonderful, Walrus?" shouted Pig. "This is the best thing that ever happened! Why I couldn't have planned it better myself!"

"What?" wailed Walrus.

"I love the rain!" shouted Pig. "It makes the plants grow and it feels so good to walk through. We can walk over to my house and have an indoor picnic. We'll dry ourselves off and listen to music and watch the rain fall and have a nice hot picnic lunch. Now doesn't that sound great?"

"I guess so," said Walrus.

"Isn't it amazing," laughed Pig, "how things always work out for the best?"

"They do?" asked Walrus.

"Of course they do, silly!" said Pig with her happiest smile. "We may be wet and hungry but we don't have to stay out in the rain and clean off the side of the bank. The wonderful rain will do it for us."

"And," laughed Pig, "I think Main Street looks great all in pink!"

"But Pig," sniffled Walrus.

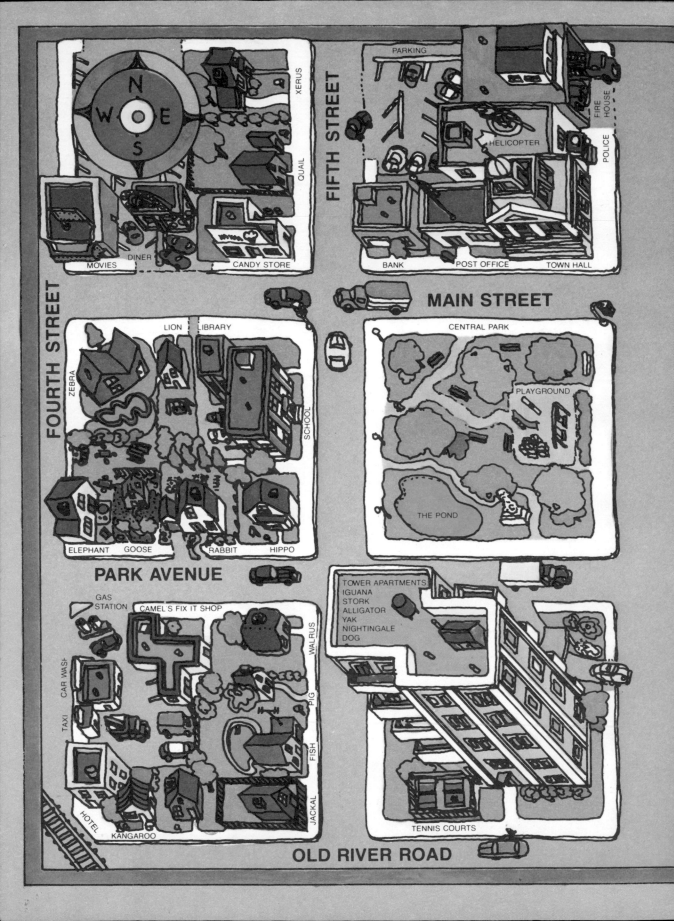